This book belongs to:

....

I am a reader and I celebrated World Book Day 2024 with this gift from my local bookseller and Oxford University Press.

WORLD BOOK DAY®

World Book Day's mission is to offer every child and young person the opportunity to read and love books by giving you the chance to have a book of your own.

To find out more, and for fun activities including video stories, audiobooks and book recommendations, visit worldbookday.com

World Book Day is a charity sponsored by National Book Tokens.

Happy
World Book Day!

When you've read this book, you can keep the fun going by swapping it, talking about it with a friend, or reading it again!

What do you want to read next? Whether it's **comics**, **audiobooks**, **recipe books** or **non-fiction** you can visit your school, local library or nearest bookshop for your next read – someone will always be happy to help.

DEAR READER,

I'm Alex, the author of this book.

I've always wanted to be a superhero. I think that's what drew me to writing Marv. You can find countless pictures of me as a child dressed up in superhero costumes.

Marv is particularly special to me because when I was growing up there weren't that many superheroes who were black and looked like me. So, it's amazing that I get the chance to write these stories, and I'm very excited for you to read them.

Marv is a story about a young boy called Marvin, who finds a super-suit in his grandad's loft, and Pixel, his robotic sidekick. His grandad used to wear the super-suit when he was a superhero back in the day! When Marvin puts on the super-suit, he becomes a superhero called Marv.

Marv's super-suit is powered by kindness and imagination. In fact, his suit only works if he's using it to try and help others. His imagination allows him to use a whole bunch of powers to stop supervillains who are trying to ruin the day.

Even more powerful than that is the greatest superpower of all, kindness. When we do good things and treat each other with kindness, I really do believe we have the power to change the world around us for the better. It's a real superpower and a power that's inside us all.

Alex

That's me!

For my cats Akira and Simone—A.F-K

For SUPER YOU, the completely marvellous reader—P.B

OXFORD
UNIVERSITY PRESS

Great Clarendon Street, Oxford OX2 6DP
Oxford University Press is a department of the University of Oxford.
It furthers the University's objective of excellence in research, scholarship,
and education by publishing worldwide. Oxford is a registered trade mark
of Oxford University Press in the UK and in certain other countries

Database right Oxford University Press (maker)

First published in 2024

British Library Cataloguing in Publication Data

Data available

ISBN: 978-0-19-279480-2

1 3 5 7 9 10 8 6 4 2

Printed in Manipal Technologies Limited, Manipal

Paper used in the production of this book is a natural,
recyclable product made from wood grown in sustainable forests.
The manufacturing process conforms to the environmental
regulations of the country of origin.

MARV
AND THE
ULTIMATE SUPERPOWER

★ FIVE ★
MINI MARV
ADVENTURES!

WRITTEN BY
ALEX FALASE-KOYA

PICTURES BY
PAULA BOWLES

OXFORD
UNIVERSITY PRESS

MARV AND THE CONJURED CHARACTERS

Marvin got down on the floor. He reached underneath a tall sweet stand, his tongue poking out of his mouth in concentration. He blindly reached around until—

'Got it!' Marvin said with a grin. He got to his feet, waving a ticket in the air.

'Thank you so much!' said a woman standing in front of Marvin. She was balancing a huge tub of popcorn, a big drink, and a hot dog awkwardly in her arms.

'No problem,' Marvin said, handing the woman's film ticket back to her. She smiled at Marvin and then made her way to one of the film screens. He slung his backpack over his shoulders. A quiet beep came from it.

'It was nice of you to help that lady with her ticket,' Marvin's grandad said, joining him in the queue at their local cinema. He was carrying a pair of tickets and some popcorn.

'I had to help! Losing a ticket and missing your film would be awful.' Marvin frowned.

'Especially when you have all your snacks lined up and ready,' Grandad agreed, pulling down his sunglasses and staring at a hot dog advert. 'So, what film are we going to see again?'

'I thought I already showed you the trailer,' Marvin said. He cocked his head sideways.

'What trailer was that then?' Grandad asked. Marvin narrowed his eyes and leaned forwards.

'You're not being serious, right?'
Marvin said.

Grandad tried to keep a straight face, but he quickly broke into a wide grin. 'You can't be talking about *The Silver Spectre, Defender of the innocent—*'

'*Keeper of the Silver Spear!*' Marvin finished. 'I knew you hadn't forgotten.'

'Of course not!'

Marvin and Grandad showed their tickets to an usher then walked towards their screen, past loads of adverts displayed for cool new films.

There was one with huge battling robots soaring through a ruined city using their rocket boosters.

Another had a scary looking shark leaping out of the water, and another showed a chaotic space battle, with

loads of spaceships shooting lasers at each other. Lastly, they walked past a bubblegum advert, where a person was blowing a bubble bigger than their head.

5

The films all looked so exciting! (Well, all of them except that shark one. That looked a bit too scary to Marvin.) This is why Marvin loved going to the cinema. The trailers and posters and popcorn—it was all so cool.

Marvin and his grandad reached the door to the screen for their film, when there was a loud crash, and then a scream.

'Stay away from the adverts!' somebody yelled.

A rumble of feet came as the other cinema-goers in the corridor started running for the exit. Marvin and Grandad turned to see what was going on and someone crashed into them, sending their popcorn flying.

'To the exit!' an usher cried as he ran too.

Why was everyone running away from the cinema? Marvin knew someone who might be able to help.

He lifted off his backpack and took a sneaky peek inside. A silvery, smooth, metallic head with round eyes peered back at him.

'Supervillain detected!' Pixel the robot beeped urgently.

Marvin gasped and looked around at the chaos. This cinema needed a superhero!

He glanced up at Grandad, who gave him a nod. Marvin took a deep breath and then ran off to the loo to change. As soon as he got into his cubicle, he threw open his backpack.

'I was looking forward to watching

that new *Silver Spectre* film,' Pixel beeped sadly as she hovered out of Marvin's bag. Pixel was Marvin's robot sidekick and more than that, she was his friend.

'So was I!' Marvin exclaimed as he pulled his super-suit out of his backpack. He never went anywhere without his superhero outfit and Pixel, just in case. Marvin got changed and, just like that, Marvin became . . . superhero Marv!

Marv and Pixel rushed back out of the toilets. Almost immediately, they bumped into another person wearing a super-suit not too different to Marv's.

'Finding the supervillain wasn't too difficult,' Marv said to Pixel.

'Yes, supervillains normally take longer to track down,' Pixel replied.

'True. They also—'

'Stop talking about me like I'm not here!' the supervillain said, stomping her feet. 'I'm the Conjurer, and it seems as though you're underestimating me. Well, let's see how you deal with the power of my imagination!'

The power of imagination? Marv frowned. His super-suit was powered by imagination too.

The Conjurer reached out towards one of the film adverts on the wall. Her hand reached it and carried on straight through—right inside!

'I hope you like sharks!' she grunted. She yanked her arm back out of the advert, and this time she was pulling something out with her. It was a shark!

Marv's tummy did multiple backflips, and he gulped hard.

The shark's jaws snapped open and shut as it wiggled forwards, and then burst out of the poster altogether. The Conjurer ran away, cackling as the shark finally emerged from the wall and launched itself at Marv, swimming through the air as if it were in water.

'ARGH!!!!'

Marv's super-suit crackled with super-speed, and he zoomed out of the way. The shark flipped back into the air and swam along, crashing into the sweet stand and snapping its jaws left and right.

Marv scrambled to his feet. He needed to use his super-suit if he was going to stop this shark from causing any more damage. He closed his eyes to think, and then he got it! The bubblegum advert!

'IT'S SUPER-SUIT TIME!' Marv declared and he placed a hand on the 'M' on his suit. 'Super-suit, please help me blow bubbles.'

A rumbling came from Marv's left sleeve, and then a large bubble blower emerged from the wrist of his suit. He pulled it up to his mouth, took a deep

breath, and blew into it as hard as he could.

A bubble, bigger than any Marv had ever seen before, grew out of the bubble blower. The shark was swimming closer but Marv stood his ground. He had to wait for just the right moment.

'NOW!' screeched Pixel.

Marv gave the bubble an extra hard blow of air and it shot towards the shark. Even though the shark snapped at it, the bubble didn't burst. Instead, the bubble stretched like elastic round the shark, until it was trapped inside and floating up to the ceiling.

'Go, Marv, go!' Pixel cheered.

Marv knew this was far from over. He spun around and spotted the Conjurer. She was in front of the space battle

poster, with her arm outstretched towards it. 'Let's see how you deal with this!' she cackled.

'Marv, according to my calculations there's a 99% chance that the Conjurer's powers come from that.' Pixel pointed at a thick, glowing bracelet on the Conjurer's wrist.

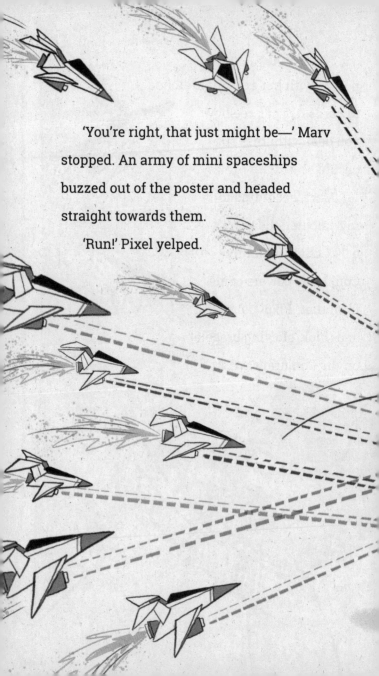

'You're right, that just might be—' Marv stopped. An army of mini spaceships buzzed out of the poster and headed straight towards them.

'Run!' Pixel yelped.

'Ouch,' Marv cried as he leaped back, trying to dodge the lasers. But it was no use, he was peppered with tiny laser beams. It felt like being pricked with a bunch of pins.

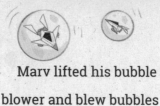

Marv lifted his bubble blower and blew bubbles towards the spaceships, but it didn't work this time. The spaceships just wove around them, dodging the bubbles with ease.

'Pixel, I need your help,' he cried.

Marv continued making the bubbles and Pixel joined him, transforming her hands into mini-fans and directing the bubbles exactly where they needed to go. The spaceships were no match for Marv and Pixel working together, and soon they were all inside the bubbles and floating to the ceiling to join the shark.

Marv let out a sigh of relief.

'The Conjurer's over there!' Pixel shouted, pointing. The Conjurer was dashing towards another advert. Marv gulped. He needed to catch her quickly. Who knew what she could let loose next?

'Suit! Please activate net mode,' Marv said. A big net sprang out of the wrist of his suit and shot out towards the Conjurer, just as she touched the advert.

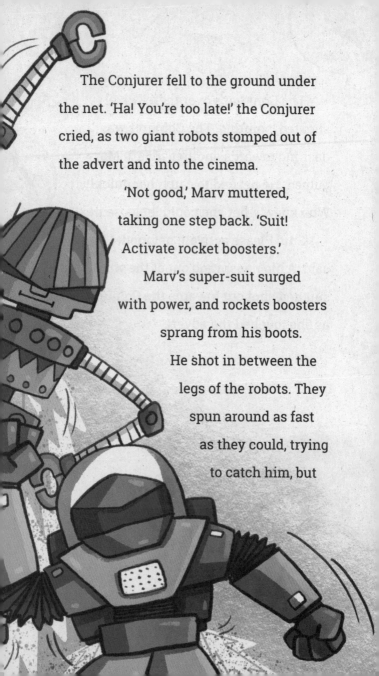

The Conjurer fell to the ground under the net. 'Ha! You're too late!' the Conjurer cried, as two giant robots stomped out of the advert and into the cinema.

'Not good,' Marv muttered, taking one step back. 'Suit! Activate rocket boosters.'

Marv's super-suit surged with power, and rockets boosters sprang from his boots. He shot in between the legs of the robots. They spun around as fast as they could, trying to catch him, but they moved so fast that they crashed into each other!

Sparks began to fly from the robots. They began to move in an awkward, jittery way. They weren't chasing after Marv any more. They charged across the room in random directions, as though they were malfunctioning.

One was heading straight for the Conjurer! Marv glanced at the robot's heavy feet, and then back to the Conjurer, trapped by the net. She couldn't get away. There was only one thing to do.

'Suit, please deactivate net!' Marv cried. The net loosened and the Conjurer rolled out of the way, just as the robot's foot crashed down on the net.

The Conjurer looked over at Marv, gave him a quick nod, and then ran away.

Marv smiled.

A beeping Pixel swooped down to where the Conjurer had been, and picked something up from the floor. A bracelet. It must have come loose when the Conjurer was trapped. Now that the Conjurer had lost the source of her power, the characters from the adverts had all disappeared, even the robots, the trapped shark, and spaceships! Marv's empty bubbles popped all around them.

Marv wiped the sweat off his brow.

'Thanks Pixel,' Marv said, jogging over.

Grandad stepped out from behind a toppled-over sweet stand.

'You were here the whole time?' Marv asked.

Grandad smiled. 'Just in case you needed me. But I could see you had everything under control, as usual!'

'I know I let the Conjurer go, but sometimes supervillains need help too,' Marv grinned. 'Now let's get this place cleaned up—we've got a film to watch!'

PIXEL TO THE RESCUE

Marvin sneezed so loudly and forcefully it made his bed shake. Grandad lifted a half-eaten bowl of chicken soup off Marvin's lap.

'I'll read you a story if you like,' said Pixel, opening a book.

'Thanks, Pixel, but I think I just need a nap,' said Marvin, coughing.

'You'll feel better after a sleep, little one.' Grandad leaned in close to Marvin and pressed the back of his hand to Marvin's warm forehead. 'Come on, Pixel, we should let Marvin get some rest.'

'I thought maybe I could stay here, just in case he wakes up and needs anything,' Pixel said.

'What a kind robot you are,' Grandad smiled. 'All right, I'll be back later to check on both of you.'

'OK.' Marvin yawned and then slumped down further into bed.

Grandad left the room, pulling the door closed behind him.

Pixel hovered next to Marvin's bed, alert.

Marvin was soon snoring softly . . . when Pixel heard something else.

A buzzing noise.

Pixel whizzed

around to see a

big fly dart through the open window. It buzzed across the room towards Marvin. He began to stir, tossing and turning in bed, murmuring to himself.

Pixel beeped.

'SUPERVIL—' Pixel slammed her hands over her mouth, stopping her trademark supervillain alarm from ringing out. She couldn't risk waking Marvin, not when he was sick. She'd have to deal with this fly alone.

Pixel lowered her hands from her mouth and narrowed her eyes. Her hands turned into fly swatters. It was time to get rid of this pesky beast! She flew at the fly, swatting at it, but the fly was speedy and dodged out of the way with ease. Worst of all, it would not stop buzzing!

Time to take things up a notch.

Pixel activated her eye lasers, setting them to stun. She focused on the fly, took aim, and then—BLAST! The buzzing stopped! Pixel swooped up and down, doing a silent little victory dance. But wait! What was that?

BUZZZZzz...

Pixel whipped around to see the fly hovering over Marvin's bookshelf! Pixel blasted at it again, this time with a flurry of lasers, but they all missed, hitting the shelf instead. A bunch of books clattered to the ground with a ...

CRASH!

'What's happening?' Marvin mumbled, sitting up in bed with a startled look on his face.

'Erm . . . nothing,' Pixel said, narrowing her eyes as the fly buzzed back out of the window. It spun around in a circle before it left. Was that a victory dance of its own?!

GRANDAD AND THE DUCK OF DOOM

'Grandad, can you please tell me a story?' Marvin asked. He was sitting at the dinner table waiting for Grandad to serve up.

'Are you sure?' Grandad said, carrying over two plates of steaming hot food. He placed them on the table and sat down with a mischievous grin. 'I don't know if I have any stories left to tell.'

'You definitely do! You were Marv before me. You wore the super-suit for years and must have had so many adventures!' Marvin said.

'Well, maybe I do have one story that I haven't told you yet,' Grandad said, stroking his beard.

'Please tell me!' Marvin begged.

'All right, all right. I'll tell you about one of the fiercest and most dangerous villains I ever faced,' Grandad began. Marvin leaned in, on the edge of his seat. 'Professor Feather,' Grandad said.

'Professor Feather? To be honest, Grandad, that doesn't sound that dangerous,' Marvin said, sitting back in his chair and raising his eyebrows.

'You mustn't judge a book by its cover, Marvin. Names can be deceiving.' Grandad pulled down his sunglasses and gave Marvin a wink. 'You see, Professor Feather built a very powerful robot . . . the Duck of Doom.'

'The Duck of Doom?' Marvin's eyebrows rose even higher.

'I know, ducks don't sound that dangerous, but—'

'Names can be deceiving,' Marvin nodded.

'Exactly. This robot was shaped like an enormous duck, and it waddled through town causing all sorts of damage,' Grandad said. 'Cars were smashed, buildings were

35

pushed over! Professor Feather was riding on its back at the controls ...'

'And that's when you stepped in,' Marvin added.

'Well, I didn't really step in. I actually flew in using a rocket-booster backpack. Pixel was with me too,' Grandad smiled.

Professor Feather was standing on the giant Duck of Doom, tapping rapidly at the controls. "Let's see how you deal with the Duck of Doom's PECK MODE!" he said.

The giant robo-duck rapidly pecked its beak at me and Pixel, trying to bring us down. We swerved out of the way of the ginormous duck beak, but that wasn't the end of the Duck of Doom. It opened its mouth and a powerful QUACK erupted from it.

It was so loud that it sent ripples through the air, knocking me and Pixel to the ground.

"Ha! Have a taste of the sonic quack!" Professor Feather cackled.

I lay on my back, feeling groggy. Pixel grabbed me by the shoulders and shook me urgently.

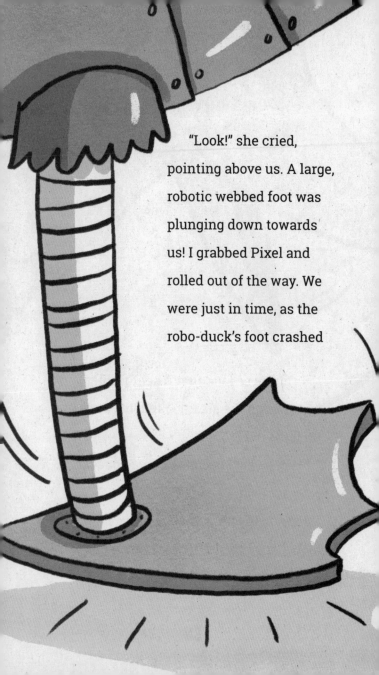

"Look!" she cried, pointing above us. A large, robotic webbed foot was plunging down towards us! I grabbed Pixel and rolled out of the way. We were just in time, as the robo-duck's foot crashed to the pavement, cracking the concrete right next to Marv's head!

"Maybe we've finally met our match," I said. "The Duck of Doom is just too powerful." Pixel and I watched in awe while the Duck of Doom stomped past us as if we weren't even there.

"Not for us! If we face it together, we can come up with a plan," Pixel said.

I nodded. "That's what you always say!"

We put our heads together, whispering.

"That's it!" I cried.

Pixel zoomed away, catching up to the Duck of Doom and zipping around and in between the robot's legs at great speed. The Duck of Doom waddled back and forth, trying to squish Pixel, but the little robot was just too fast.

While the robo-duck was distracted, I flew up behind it and put my arms together.

"Suit! Please activate sonic wave!" I said.

Energy gathered from all over my suit into my hands and then blasted forwards. The shock wave whooshed towards the Duck of Doom. BOOM! The wave hit it, and the Duck of Doom toppled to the ground with a great CRASH. I gave a sigh of relief—it was finally over.

Professor Feather crawled out from the wreckage. "Noooo! My beautiful Duck of Doom!" he cried, throwing himself over his invention.

I approached Professor Feather. "Suit! Please activate tissue mode."

Professor Feather sniffed and took the tissue from me. "Thanks."

☆ ✳ ✺ ✳

'So, what happened to Professor Feather?' Marvin asked when Grandad finished his story.

'Professor Feather put his villainous ways behind him,' Grandad said. 'Nowadays, we go bowling together on Thursdays.'

JOE, EVA, AND THE KILLER PLANTS

Eva and Joe looked around in dismay at the place that had once been their happy school playground. Now, it was overrun with giant vines and massive Venus flytraps. Everything had been fine until that supervillain, Violet Vine, had shown up, and got to work on her evil plans to take over the school.

Luckily, Marv was already on the case.

'Eva and Joe—can you team up and rescue your classmates from these dastardly plants? I'm going to put a stop to Violet Vine!' And with that, Marv was off, running towards the school building after the supervillain.

Joe and Eva looked at each other and then at the chaos around them.

'We can do this, right?' Joe said nervously.

'Maybe,' Eva replied.

'Help!' One of Joe and Eva's

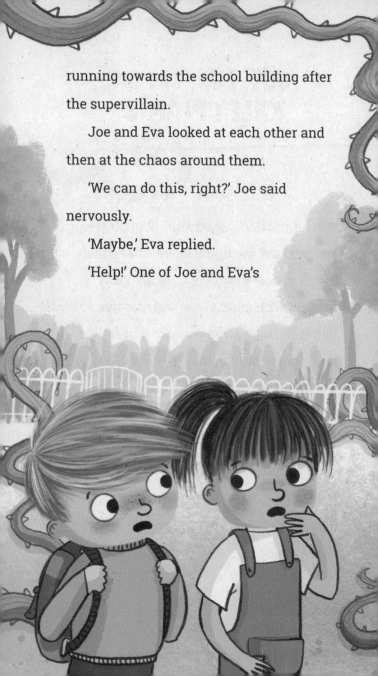

classmates was hanging upside down, held in the mouth of a Venus flytrap. There was no time to lose!

Joe lifted a nearby watering can in his trembling hands. He swung it back and then tossed it wildly towards the plant.

The watering can spiralled up towards the Venus flytrap. CLANG! The plant dropped the kid from its clutches.

'Did I hit it?' Joe gasped, peeking nervously through his fingers.

'Yeah, you did—you're a hero!' Eva cried.

Joe grinned. 'We can do this!'

'Yes, we can,' Eva nodded.

The friends got to work, pulling apart vines and dragging their classmates out of slobbering Venus flytraps. With

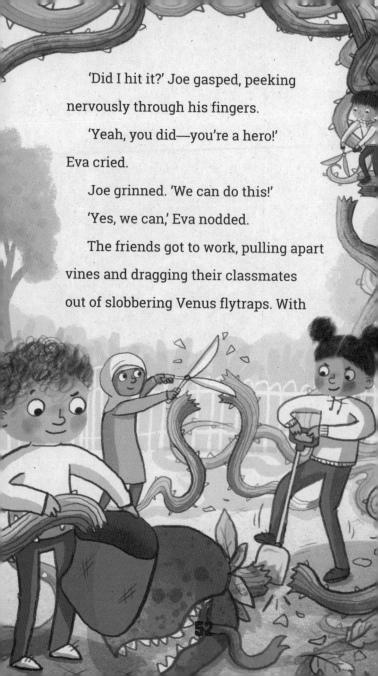

each classmate they saved, their band of friends grew bigger. In no time at all, they were a force to be reckoned with, even without superpowers!

'Look!' cried Joe. The crew looked into the sky and watched Marv defeating Violet Vine and saving the day.

'I wish Marvin could have seen this,' said Joe, smiling. 'I wonder where he is . . .'

CONJURING UP SOME KINDNESS

A gloved hand knocked on the front door of a house. A little girl opened it. She had a wide, toothy smile.

'Hello, Yaz,' she said. 'Did you forget your key?'

'You're not supposed to call me that! I have a secret identity to protect, you know,' the person whispered as they stepped inside.

'OK, sorry,' the little girl said. 'Hello, Conjurer.'

'That's more like it!' the Conjurer said as she walked into the living room and flopped down on the couch.

'How did causing chaos at the cinema

go?' the little girl asked, sitting next to her.

'Euurgh, I don't want to talk about it,'
the Conjurer groaned, looking down at her
boots.

'Oh . . . OK,' the little girl sniffed.

The Conjurer looked up. 'Actually, I got
saved by a superhero, if you can believe it.'

'A superhero helped you?!' the girl said.

'Yep! He didn't have to be kind, but he

was . . . ' the Conjurer laughed and put an arm around the little girl. 'Anyway, thanks to him I get to spend the rest of the day with you. Do you have the popcorn ready?'

'Are you sure you want to watch a film? Even after what happened today?' the little girl asked.

'Of course!' the Conjurer replied, giving the small girl a big hug. 'I've always got time for my little sister!'

HERE ARE SOME IDEAS TO HELP YOU UNLOCK THE ULTIMATE SUPERPOWER

My super-suit gives me unlimited powers. I can fly through the air with rocket boosters or move at super-speed. But there's one power my suit doesn't generate, the ultimate superpower—kindness. It's a power you don't need a super-suit for—it's inside all of us. We just have to choose to use it and by being thoughtful and considerate towards those around us, we can make the world a better place every single day.

HELP OTHERS

If you see someone in need, ask if they'd like some help—this can be something small like picking up someone's dropped film ticket or offering a tissue.

SAY SOMETHING

If you think something nice about a person, say it. For example, if you think your friend is great at video games, tell them.

INCLUDE OTHERS

No one likes to be left out. When you're playing a game, try to make sure everyone who wants to join in is invited.

LOOK AFTER THE PLANET

Caring for the Earth can take many forms, from watering plants and feeding the birds to sorting the recycling and remembering to switch off lights.

LISTEN

When someone is talking to you or telling you a joke or story, listening to them shows that you care.

BE POLITE

Saying 'please' and 'thank you' is an easy way to show gratitude.

LOOK OUT FOR OTHERS

If someone is going through a hard time or being bullied, try to stand up for them and be there to listen to their problems.

LOOK AFTER YOURSELF

Remember to be kind to yourself. Speak to yourself positively and rest when you need to.

ABOUT THE AUTHOR

ALEX FALASE-KOYA

Alex is a London native. He has been writing children's fiction since he was a teenager and was a winner of Spread the Word's 2019 London Writers Awards for YA and Children's. He co-wrote The Breakfast Club Adventures, the first fiction series by Marcus Rashford. He now lives in Walthamstow with his girlfriend and two cats.

ABOUT THE ILLUSTRATOR

PAULA BOWLES

Paula grew up in Hertfordshire, and has always loved drawing, reading, and using her imagination, so she studied illustration at Falmouth College of Arts and became an illustrator. She now lives in Bristol, and has worked as an illustrator for over ten years, and has had books published with Nosy Crow, Simon and Schuster and Oxford University Press.

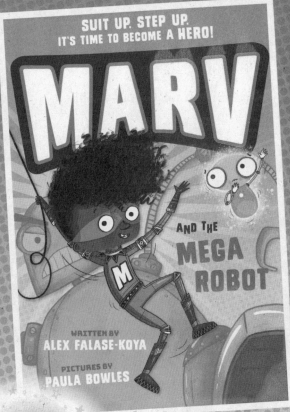

SUIT UP. STEP UP.
IT'S TIME TO BECOME A **HERO!**

MARV

AND THE
**MEGA
ROBOT**

WRITTEN BY
ALEX FALASE-KOYA

PICTURES BY
PAULA BOWLES

At home, Grandad put some music on while he made dinner. He left his thick sunglasses on even though they were inside.

'Hey Grandad,' Marv said.

'Hey little one,' Grandad replied.

'You know it's the Science Fair tomorrow? Me and Joe are entering our robot, but it broke again today. It might have exploded, but only a little bit … It's not really dangerous or anything, I promise,' Marvin added quickly.

'Nothing wrong with a little bit of danger every now and again.' Grandad pulled down his sunglasses and winked. Marvin giggled, then stopped. A memory from earlier was in his head.

'A kid in our class was mean about our invention. I told Joe not to worry about it, but maybe I should have done more. Maybe I should have—'

Grandad raised a hand, interrupting Marvin.

'Come over here,' Grandad said. Marvin got up and walked towards him. Grandad wrapped Marvin up in a warm hug. 'The heroic thing isn't to start a fight, it's to be a good friend, and that's what you did.' Grandad let go, then reached out

and patted Marvin's chest. 'Your big heart, little one. That's your superpower.'

'Can that really be a superpower?' Marvin said with a smile, staring up at Grandad.

'Of course, it can. And I think you'd make a great superhero one day.' Grandad pulled down his sunglasses and gave another wink.

'But superheroes don't even exist any more.'

'That is true.' Grandad looked at Marvin and grinned. 'But maybe it's time for that to change ... Could you do me a favour, Marvin? Go into the loft and bring down my old brown suitcase. I have some keepsakes in there I want to share with you.'

Feeling puzzled, Marvin went upstairs, then up the thin ladder into the loft. It was dark and filled with cobwebs and dusty boxes. He had no idea how many spiders or other creepy-crawlies were up here. Part of him wanted to leave, but Grandad only asked him to get the suitcase. He couldn't turn back without even trying.

Marvin took a couple of steps,
then his foot hit something, and he
almost fell.

Grandad's brown suitcase lay
at Marvin's feet, covered in a thick
layer of dust. Marvin tried to lift it,
but it was surprisingly heavy. He
shook it, and it rattled. What was
inside? There was only one way to
find out.

Marvin reached down and opened the suitcase. Inside was a piece of clothing. Marvin held it up ... It was a dull blue colour with a huge 'M' on the front. His jaw dropped. It looked a bit like a superhero outfit!

CHAPTER 2

The super-suit looked way too big for Marvin, but he couldn't resist. He had to try it on!

Marvin slipped the suit on over his clothes. The long fabric of the legs and arms flopped over his hands and feet. Marvin laughed; he was practically drowning in the suit. Just as he was about to take it off, the super-suit suddenly changed. Its arms and legs shrunk until they were exactly Marvin's size. He stared at the suit in amazement. It fit him perfectly now.

World Book Day is about changing lives through reading

When you **choose to read** in your spare time it makes you

Feel happier	Better at reading	More successful

Find your **reading superpower** by

1. Listening to books being read aloud (or listening to audiobooks)

2. Having books at home

3. Choosing the books YOU want to read

4. Asking for ideas on what to read next

5. Making time to read

6. Finding ways to make reading FUN!

SPONSORED BY

NATIONAL BOOK Tokens

Changing lives through a love of books and reading.

World Book Day® is a charity sponsored by National Book Tokens

ILLUSTRATED BY VIVIAN TRUONG

LOVE MARV?
WHY NOT TRY THESE TOO . . . ?